I Want a Dog for Christmas, Charlie Brown!

 LITTLE SIMON

An imprint of Simon & Schuster Children's Publishing Division
1230 Avenue of the Americas, New York, New York 10020
Copyright © 2004 by United Feature Syndicate, Inc. All rights reserved.
PEANUTS is a registered trademark of United Feature Syndicate, Inc.
LITTLE SIMON is a registered trademark of Simon & Schuster, Inc., and associated
colophon is a trademark of Simon & Schuster, Inc.
All rights reserved, including the right of reproduction in whole or in part in any form.
Manufactured in China
ISBN-13: 978-1-4169-1380-1
ISBN-10: 1-4169-1380-7

I Want a Dog for Christmas, Charlie Brown!

Adapted by Jim Thomas
Illustrated by Tom Brannon
Based on the television special produced by Lee Mendelson and Bill Melendez

LITTLE SIMON
New York   London   Toronto   Sydney

It was Christmas vacation, and Linus and Lucy's little brother, Rerun, was looking for something to do. He rang the doorbell at Charlie Brown's house. He had a basketball and a bag of Christmas cookies with him. Charlie Brown opened the door.

"Ask your dog if he wants to come out and shoot a few baskets," Rerun said.

"I'll see if I can find him," said Charlie Brown.

Charlie Brown disappeared back into the house. Suddenly Snoopy burst through the door and grabbed the basketball right out of Rerun's hands!

Snoopy dribbled to the basket and made a shot. He caught the ball, spun, and made another. Snoopy was a basketball whirlwind! Then Snoopy dribbled back to Rerun, flipped him the ball, and went back into the house.

After a moment Charlie Brown came back to the door.

"I couldn't find him," Charlie Brown said. "But I doubt he would have been interested."

But Rerun wasn't about to give up. "Ask your dog if he wants to come out and just *play*. Afterward I'll give him a Christmas cookie with sprinkles."

Inside, Snoopy heard what Rerun said.

And he liked what he heard!

Rerun and Snoopy played all day. They danced.
They jumped. They tumbled and sang.

Finally they collapsed into a heap, laughing. Rerun opened his brown paper bag and handed a Christmas cookie to Snoopy. Snoopy happily scarfed it down.

Then Snoopy grabbed the entire bag and ran off!
"I guess dogs eat a lot!" Rerun said.

The next day Rerun went back to Charlie Brown's house. Charlie Brown opened the door.

"Please ask your dog to come out and play again," Rerun said hopefully.

"Why don't you get your own dog?" Charlie Brown asked.

Rerun looked sad. "My mom won't let me. She says dogs are too much trouble."

"That's too bad," Charlie Brown said.

Rerun started to walk home. "There's only one thing left to do," he said. "It's time to see Santa Claus!" Rerun saw Lucy. He called out to her, "I need you to take me to Santa Claus."

"Why?" Lucy asked.

"I have something very important to ask him," he said.

Meanwhile Snoopy was up to something. He was searching through all the stuff in his doghouse.

Finally he came out with a box. He pulled out a furry red coat, a long red hat, a pair of black boots, and a fake beard. He put everything on. Now he was dressed like Santa! He pulled a bell out of the box and started ringing it.

Lucy and Rerun walked up. Lucy looked Snoopy over doubtfully. "Okay, if you're a real Santa Claus, where are your reindeer?" she asked.

Snoopy just rang his bell.

"How are you going to land on all those rooftops," Lucy went on, "and go down all those chimneys? And after you go down a chimney, how are you going to get back up, huh? I'll give you about three houses, and then you'll be completely exhausted."

Suddenly Snoopy stuck his bell onto Lucy's face. It stayed there!

With a *pop,* Lucy pulled the bell off her face. She glared at Snoopy, then turned to Rerun.

"As your big sister," Lucy said, "I feel it is my duty to tell you that what you see is *not* the real Santa Claus. What you're looking at is a dog in a Santa Claus suit! Now that I've told you this, how does it make you feel?"

Rerun grabbed Snoopy and gave him a big hug. "I like him!" he said. "I don't care who he is as long as he can get me a dog for Christmas."

Snoopy rang his bell and pointed at the box where he'd kept his Santa outfit.

"What does he want?" Rerun asked Lucy.

"I think he wants a contribution in his box there," said Lucy.

Rerun reached into his pocket, got out a coin, and flipped it into Snoopy's box. Snoopy shook Rerun's hand excitedly and said, "Woof!"

Lucy pulled Rerun away. Snoopy waved good-bye with his bell.

"What did he say?" Lucy asked her little brother.

"He said, 'Thank you,'" said Rerun. "'The money is for a worthy cause. Merry Christmas. And say hello to the stupid kid with the blanket and his crabby sister.'"

Lucy's face turned red. Snoopy was talking about her and Linus!

"Forget it," Lucy said to Rerun. "Mom will never let you have a dog anyway. They can be a lot of trouble. Just ask Charlie Brown about his stupid dog!"

Rerun found Charlie Brown and Snoopy out by Snoopy's doghouse. Charlie Brown handed a letter to Snoopy. "This letter came for you today," he said.

Snoopy opened the letter and started to read. He smiled. Then he started to laugh!
He handed the letter back to Charlie Brown. Charlie Brown looked it over.

"It's a letter to Snoopy from his brother, Spike," Charlie Brown explained. "The one who lives in the desert."

"Does Spike live all alone in the desert?" Rerun asked.

"Yes, he does," said Charlie Brown. "He's probably very lonely."

Suddenly Rerun had a great idea!

Rerun asked Snoopy to write a letter for him. Snoopy whipped out his typewriter and put a piece of paper in it.

"Please write to your brother in the desert," Rerun said. "Tell him he can be my dog."

Snoopy typed as Rerun talked.

"Tell him we'll be pals. He can chase sticks and pull me in my wagon and learn tricks. And we'll celebrate Christmas together!"

When Spike arrived he was carrying a cactus! Snoopy, Charlie Brown, Lucy, and Rerun went out to meet him. Snoopy and Spike were so happy to see each other, they started dancing!

Lucy said, "Spike! Good grief, you're so thin! I'm going to take you home and feed you."

Lucy did just that. She fed him milk shakes to fatten him up and took extra-special care of him.
"Hey! That's my blanket he's wearing!" Linus cried.
Lucy was dressed as a nurse. "It's a hospital robe!" she explained.

When Spike was feeling better Rerun taught him lots of games, and they had fun together.
But Rerun's mother wouldn't let Spike stay, so he had to go back to the desert.

With tears in his eyes, Rerun gave Spike a big hug. "Good-bye!" he said. "I'll really miss you!
Don't forget to write!"

Spike waved, picked up his cactus, and started back home.

"Rerun," Lucy said. She held a piece of paper in her hand. "I realize how upset you must be about losing Spike. So to make you forget about him, I've signed you up to be in our Christmas play."

Lucy handed the piece of paper to Rerun. "Here's the script. Just memorize it."

Rerun panicked. "But I can't read!" he cried.

"Don't worry," Lucy said. "You only have one line. I'll help you."

On the night of the play the gang stood together. Rerun stood at the edge of the group. He was nervous. Each of the kids told part of the story. Schroeder began. "We are here to tell you of a wondrous light," he said.

"A wondrous light that was a star," said Linus.

Lucy said, "The wise men saw the star and followed it from afar."

Then Charlie Brown said, "They found the stable in the night, beneath the star so big and bright."

Rerun nudged his sister. "I can't remember my line!" he whispered out of the corner of his mouth.

Franklin spoke. "The wise men left the presents there. Gifts so precious and rare."
Pig Pen said, "Look up, look up, the star still stands, seen by millions in the lands."
It was time for Rerun's line!
"You better remember it right now," Lucy hissed, "or else!"
Suddenly Rerun stood straight up. "The star that shone at Bethlehem still shines for us today!" he yelled.
Out of the corner of her mouth, Lucy whispered, "Merry Christmas!"
Rerun felt faint. He'd done it! "Thank you!" he whispered to Lucy.